HOW THE WIND PLAYS

for
Otis!
Daniel Kirk

MICHAEL LIPSON   ILLUSTRATIONS BY **DANIEL KIRK**

HYPERION BOOKS FOR CHILDREN

NEW YORK

Text © 1994 by Michael Lipson.
Illustrations © 1994 by Daniel Kirk.
All rights reserved. Printed in Hong Kong by
South China Printing Co. (1988) LTD.
For information address
Hyperion Books for Children,
114 Fifth Avenue,
New York, New York 10011.
FIRST EDITION
1 3 5 7 9 10 8 6 4 2
Library of Congress Cataloging-in-Publication Data
Lipson, Michael.
How the wind plays/Michael Lipson; illustrated by Daniel Kirk
—1st ed.
p.   cm.
Summary: The wind, in the form of a mischievous child, indulges in
such playful antics as shaking tree branches against windows and
blowing snow inside.
ISBN 1-56282-325-6 (trade)—ISBN 1-56282-326-4 (lib. bdg.)
[1. Winds—Fiction.]   I. Kirk, Daniel, ill.   II. Title.
PZ7.L6695Ho   1994
[E]—dc20   93-11742   CIP   AC

~~~

Design by Julia Gorton

The artwork for each picture is prepared using
oil paint on gessoed English watercolor paper.

This book is set in 30-point Lucian.

For Asher and Holly
—M.L.

For my parents, Don and Connie Kirk
—D.K.

*T*he wind never seems to
sit down or stand still

but is always at play.

The wind can skim sailboats across a pond

or take a kite up
higher and higher

or set a windmill spinning
with a finger flick.

The wind loves to play
with leaves from
the autumn trees

and *kick* newspapers along city streets.

In the desert,
the wind pushes sand dunes around—
just for fun.

The wind can fling down rain
or race clouds along the length of the sky.

The wind sends breezes skipping through the park

or starts a huge gale,
playing rough-and-tumble
with the waves.

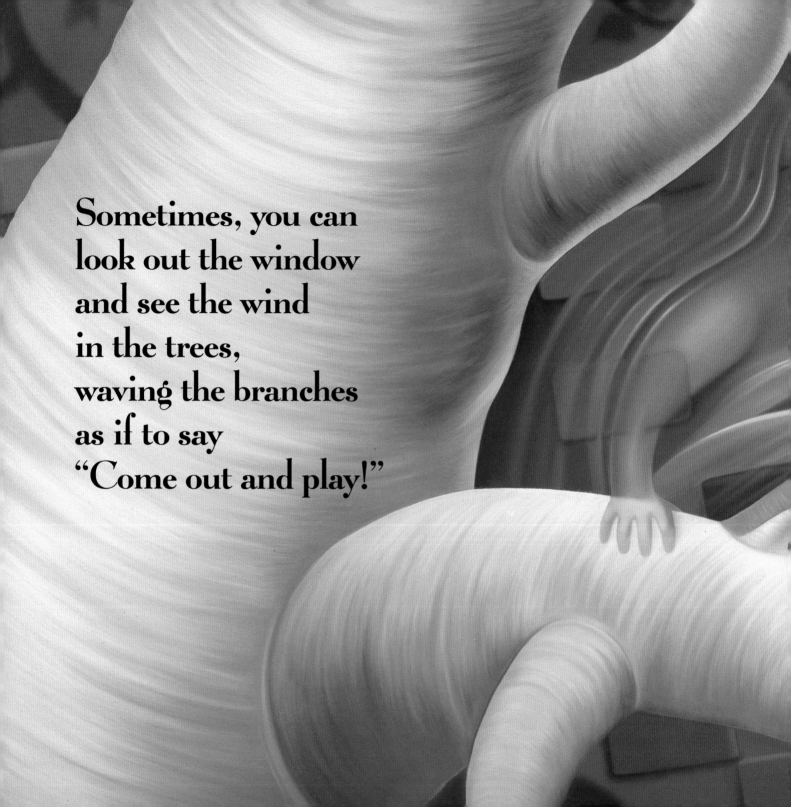

Sometimes, you can
look out the window
and see the wind
in the trees,
waving the branches
as if to say
"Come out and play!"

And, in the winter, a mischievous

wind can push snow under the windowsill.

Even on
the calmest day,
when everything
seems still,
there is always
a tiny breeze
or a gust
or a breath
as the wind sighs
and wonders
what game to play next.